EX LIBRIS

SEBASTIAN FAULKS

PISTACHE RETURNS

HUTCHINSON
LONDON

Published by Hutchinson 2016

1 3 5 7 9 10 8 6 4 2

Copyright © Sebastian Faulks 2016
Illustrations © Giorgos Papadakis 2016

Sebastian Faulks has asserted his right to be identified as the author of this
Work in accordance with the Copyright, Designs and Patents Act 1988.

First published in Great Britain in 2016 by

Hutchinson
20 Vauxhall Bridge Road
London SW1V 2SA

Hutchinson is part of the Penguin Random House group of companies
whose addresses can be found at global.penguinrandomhouse.com.

www.penguin.co.uk

A CIP catalogue record for this book is available from the British Library.

ISBN 9780091931070

Typeset in 11/14 pt Fournier MT
Jouve (UK), Milton Keynes
Printed and bound by CPI books GmbH, Leck, Germany

Penguin Random House is committed to a sustainable future for
our business, our readers and our planet. This book is made from
Forest Stewardship Council® certified paper.

MIX
From responsible
sources
FSC® C083411

Author's Note

Most of the pieces here were broadcast on the BBC Radio 4 literary quiz programme, *The Write Stuff*, between 2006 and 2015.

The programme itself ran from 1998 to 2015. It started life, along with several other hastily commissioned quizzes, as a filler for the 1.30 slot when a new controller decreed that the *World at One* should lose 15 minutes, thus leaving a half-hour gap before *The Archers*. The brainchild of question master James Walton, *The Write Stuff* was the only such quiz to survive, going on for 17 years until another decree cut off its legs in 2015.

I would like to thank all those people who have expressed their dismay at this decision; but in truth it was a pretty good run.

Some of the parodies and squibs here, e.g. Knaussgard, Marias, Hollinghurst, were not on Radio 4, but were written for this book. However, like a rock band on tour, I have been wary of playing too much from the new album and have thrown in half a dozen tracks reprised from Pistache 1, which came out ten years ago. I hope they don't seem too rusty now.

I would like to thank all the listeners who said how much they enjoyed the show; those guests (the majority) who entered into the spirit; the programme producers Sam Michel and Alexandra Smith; and the core team: Beth Chalmers, who did the readings; my inspired opposite number, John Walsh; and James Walton, whose intricate questions and patient chairing made it such fun to take part in.

SF July 2016

Modern Times

JOHN BETJEMAN
reflects on St Paul's precinct being Occupied

◄○►

In the shadow of the pillars, hard by Paternoster Square –
It was hardly Wren's intention to have vagrants camping
     there.
Whisp'ring dome and candled choir stall, chancel fabric
     starts to crack;
Where the deacon dons his surplice there's a tent from
     A. C. Black.
Driven out, the poor old deacon; Dean has followed him
     in pique
All because a bearded camper garbed investments like
     a freak
Asks the question, 'Who'll inherit?' Clearly it is *not*
     the meek.

But . . . bend your ear to Beardie's message, guaranteed to
     make you cross.
Banks are free to keep their winnings, you and I must bear
     their loss.
Shut the schools and fire the nurses, let the library close
     its door:
Bankers want three million bonus or they'll take their trade
     off shore.

Double dip in distant haven, is this how the law was bent:
Barclays on ten billion profit paying tax at one per cent?

Ghosts of Hawksmoor, Wren and Morris, Arts and Crafts,
    St Pancras high,
Come together in the forecourt, let the heavens hear you cry.
Say to Goldman, Morgan Stanley, Merrill, Lloyds and R BS :
Take your bonus, tax avoidance, greed and filth and
    fiscal mess;
Take your blackmail, coke and Porsches, let the Bishop help
    you pack;
Hail a cab for City Airport; *go* to Frankfurt, *don't* come back.

THE BRONTËS

find their various houses in The Good Hotel Guide

<u>Lowood Manor (formerly Lowood School House)</u>
'We loved it here. Mr Brocklehurst, the owner, believes that less is more and is as good as his word! Small helpings at dinner and a bracing wooden plank at bed time did me the world of good. I made friends with a sweet little maid called Jane. Sad to discover on a return visit that Mr B had to leave following outbreak of typhus and a few deaths. Health and safety gone mad!'
   Miss Helen Burns

<u>Thornfield Manor</u>
'Mr Rochester, the manager, promised me the Candlelit Dinner Option, but then seemed to have eyes only for the young governess. Very disappointing when it distinctly said NO PETS.'
   Miss Blanche Ingram

'I came here from my home in Belgium for a weekend of prayer and self-flagellation. What a *ménage*! The landlord has a mistress, two fiancées and a French child of uncertain parentage. Grace, the chambermaid, smells of sherry. Demure Miss Eyre, the governess, was more to my taste, thought the fire precautions are a scandal. The best room – in the attic – was said to be closed for refurbishment, though I distinctly heard someone moaning in it.'

Paul Emmanuel, Brussels

Wuthering Heights

A long-term *Guide* favourite, though recently some guests have complained of creaky windows and disembodied voices. Others still find the 'honesty bar' a considerable draw.

'Landlord Hindley (no relation to Moors Myra) certainly enjoys a glass! The young stable lad is a moody fellow and the housekeeper Mrs Dean a bit of a chatterbox. Avoid the room with the graffiti and the broken window pane. Since my narrative-framing duties necessitated only a short stay, I hesitate to go into detail, but I would say this: WH is not for the faint-hearted!'

Mr Lockwood

'Our slumbers were interrupted by a man with a shovel, covered from head to foot in earth. He said he had been digging up the daughter of the house, Catherine by name, for 'one last go-round'. What can you say? My husband and I find the comforts of our own dear Cranford far superior and we shall not be returning.'

Mrs E. Gaskell

'Wow, wow, wow! I've come ho-o-o-o-o-me!'
  Miss K. B., Bexleyheath, London

Haworth Parsonage B & B

'A charming taste of times gone by,' writes *Anon*. 'High tea at six, hymns round the harmonium at seven and lights out at eight. We loved the 'eat-all-you-can porridge buffet' at breakfast and the three silent waitresses who watched us from the corner of the scullery. Rooms a little on the chilly side.'

Male guests not welcome.

Wildfell Hall

A new entry in the *Guide* this year. 'Wildfell is tragically overlooked by most weekenders. Landlord Arthur Huntingdon is a bit of a 'loose cannon', to be sure, but his bar is ever open. Why not give it a go?'
  Anne B

GUSTAVE FLAUBERT

asks Bouvard and Pécuchet to update their
Dictionary of Received Ideas

The Angel of the North, The Millennium Bridge and Battersea Power Station. Call them 'iconic'. Look round for applause.

You should also apply the i-word to LP covers, TV theme tunes, popular catchphrases, famous comedy sketches – anything you like except Russian religious imagery.

The Internet. Say: 'It has given a voice to everyone.' Ignore the fact that 90 per cent of those enfranchised appear to be bag ladies or Nazis.

Your first memory. Recount what it is. Pause, and then say: 'Of course, I don't know if I *really* remember it or whether I've just been told.' Look round for admiration. If more admiration needed, say, 'Up to a point, Lord Copper.' Don't forget to look round again afterwards.

Bath or shower. Prefer shower. Say you don't like baths because you don't like to 'wallow in your own filth'. Ignore the fact that you are not a pig-farm labourer but work on a computer in a modern office.

Pall Mall and St James's clubs. Say they are 'full of old fogeys' who eat 'nursery food'. Suggest that the members go off after lunch to be spanked by their 'old nannies'.

Madonna. She does not get a new hairstyle and change of outfit between records, she 'reinvents herself'.

Some of these incarnations are 'iconic'. Be sure of which ones.

Oedipus. Say with a rueful chuckle that he was 'too fond of his mother.' Ignore the fact that he didn't know Jocasta was his mother and was so appalled when he did find out that he blinded himself.

Cricket. Call any game you happen to see 'real *England, Their England* stuff'; mention cucumber sandwiches and tea. Ignore the game's violent edge and the fact that it is chiefly played on matting in the Indian subcontinent.

Americans. Say: 'They have no sense of irony'. Ignore Woody Allen, Bart Simpson, Philip Roth, Walter Matthau, Jack Lemon, Dorothy Parker, Bob Hope, eecummings, John Updike, James Thurber, Tina Fey and Amy Poehler, the casts of *Friends*, *Cheers* and *Frasier*, Saul Bellow, Sarah Silverman, Ogden Nash, Larry David, Joan Rivers and the entire collected *New Yorker* cartoons.

Newspapers. The *Times* is 'the noticeboard of the establishment'. The *Guardian* is read by 'sandal-wearing, knit-your-own-hummus-eaters'. The 'dear old *Torygraph*' has lost its way. The *Mail* is 'beyond redemption'. You yourself read none of them, preferring to get your news 'from the Internet'. It is not necessary to be more specific.

Modern novels. You don't read them, because you prefer something with a 'proper story'.

Classic novels. You don't read them either. You prefer biographies, because they deal with 'real life'.

Politics. Boris Johnson 'adds to the gaiety of nations'. Assert that 'dear old Wedgie Benn' turned into a 'national treasure'. 'Maggie' was a 'union-basher'. Most MPs spend the day 'fiddling their expenses'. You yourself don't vote because 'they're all as bad as each other'. While propounding this view, feel free to blame 'the media'.

JONATHAN SWIFT

has a Modest Proposal for the London bicyclist

It is a melancholy object to those who walk through this great town to see the garish yellow jerkins of those upon the two-wheeled pedal-driven conveyance as they mount the walkways with no concern for the safety of the ambulant population, be they infant or advanced in years; or on the highway ford upstream against the legal flow of four-wheeled carriages which might at any moment flatten them; nor yet pause at coloured beacons posted only for their safe passage, but rather pass through with nose held high for all the world as though inviolate, not subject to the laws by which we lesser mortals must comport ourselves; and venture forth at night disdaining even rudimentary lanthorns while shaking choleric fists against the lawful citizenry.

As to my own part, I feel that this yellow-jerkined company, convinced of its superiority, should put it to the test. I propose that we withdraw our beleaguered and inadequate militias forthwith from Mesopotamia and the poppy fields of the Pathan tribesmen, bring them and their feeble blunderbusses home; and in their place that we dispatch six yellow-jerkined companies upon their two-wheeled conveyances to ride full tilt against the enemy cohorts.

For being immune from ordinary danger, such inviolable and superior troops could surely bring home the victory that has eluded our more conventional cavalry these many years. And for provisioning such a force would need but little: a puncturing repair device for each man would render unnecessary the behemoth of the King's ordnance; while for lethal weaponry, what could be more effective in the war against the lesser races than the adamantine power of the two-wheeled cavalry's self-admiring sneer?

A. A. MILNE

gets gritty

Little boy kneels at the foot of the bed,
One nasal piercing in one little head.
Hush, hush, whisper who dare,
Christopher Robin hasn't a prayer.

Peep through my fingers, what do I see?
Hot naked ladies on Murdoch TV.
Wearing a dressing gown, reading a mag,
There's Mummy's partner having a fag.

God bless Daddy, wherever he is,
It's five years now since he gave me a kiss.
Oh Lord, don't forget to make me look cool,
Stealing Toyotas and bunking off school.

Bright golden curls on a bright little bonce,
Grandma's a pusher and uncle's a nonce.
Give me a PlayStation, Game Cube at least,
Big Macs and Pringles for my midnight feast.

Lord, let the Social send a man round,
Get me out of this tower block, down to the ground.
Hush, hush, whisper who dare,
Christopher Robin has gone into care.

MARK TWAIN

tires of the Mississippi and sends Huck Finn up the Thames

My Pap beat me so often I got taken away and this care home chief Mrs Douglas tried to git me do GCSE and stuff. Pap said if he saw me near any schoolhouse he'd tan my back end with the hick'ry so good be the colour of a cotton wood tree. I was playin hooky eight days a week and I don't put no stock in learnin'. This Douglas **** she told me I was goin' to a bad place so I smoked some more weed in mah pipe and it warn't long before I lit out one night and found mahself down on the river – near Teddington with mah friend Jim who was one big bad ******. We formed an ambuscade just near Hampton Court and stole a motor skiff, a reeeeal river boat, and headed her upstream. Jus' then we saw a sign for Kempton Races.

'Hey, de Camptown Races,' said Jim, 'we gwyne sing all night, gwyne sing all day.'

I told him to lay down and pick some cotton. Next thing I know we was passing through some place called Eton.

'Hey man, why de kids all dress' up like penguin?' said Jim. 'Why dey am got no chin?'

'Maybe and it's a charm to keep away the Devil,' I said, and I sho' nuff clumb up the mast of the skiff like Ah seen a ghost. Them boys was scarin' me good, Ah doan min' tellin' you. With them tailcoat and stiff collars they was like zombies from the dead.

Next day we tied up on a tow head in a place called Cookham.

'Maybe we get some roasted hog here in Cook Ham, boss,' said Jim. 'And some grits.'

He was always thinkin' about his belly tho we had a fifty-pound sack of cornmeal in the bilges and a four-gallon jug of whisky. We din' find no hogs nor no bacon neither in Cookham, only thing they had was some paintings by some man called Spencer, said the Lord came back in Cookham. I don't put no stock by religion and I knew that was moonshine.

Next day we steamed in somewhere they was rowin' little punts eight at a time. It was called Henley. There was ole boys in stripe jackets pink and gold and they was shoutin' at us. 'Kindly clear the course, the regatta is under way.'

'What dey talkin' 'bout re-gatta?' said Jim. 'Ah's gonna kick their sorry ass with mah motor skiff. Dere's gon be only one winner here, boss.'

We was just comin' near the finish line with all them flags like jack o' lanterns or lightnin' bugs by the riverside taverns and this man comes on board and put Jim in cuffs round his wrists.

'Don't worry, my friend,' I said, 'I don't think in Hen-lee they ever seed a ******.'

PHILIP LARKIN

prepares lines in celebration of the Queen Mother's
115th Birthday

They mucked you up, your Mum- and Dad-in-law;
And then the lisping brother and his Yankee bitch:
For them the plane trees and the parties by the Seine;
For you the chores, the kiddies and the Blitz,
Snagging your slightly-outmoded shoes on the rubble
Of Mrs Snotweed's privy in what's left of Bethnal Green.

In the back seat of the hearse-like Daimler going home,
You scan the *Evening News* to see the outcome
Of your five-bob treble in the last at Haydock Park.
Another Railway Arms slides past, its table d'hôte a pie,
Stewed pears, pale ale and something final in the dark.

In castle corridors the draught disturbs dead forebears,
Balmoral princes in their lifeless gilt.
You cut the ribbon at the local 'media studies' centre;
A dozen sycophants grow flushed on Tesco's Riesling;
Your mincing courtiers make jokes about the kilt.

But Christmas time: your daughter mumming on
the idiot box,
'My husband and I . . .' – a phrase long lost to *you* . . .
Loneliness revives: the slice of lemon,
Three good goes of gin – and somewhere, beyond
the battlement,
A white moon glows; and you almost immortal, mortal too.

H. G. WELLS
made many predictions, few of which came true*

◄○►

In 1979 a female politician stood for the office of prime minister of the United Kingdom, but was soundly defeated at the polls. In the following years women withdrew from the work place altogether and by 1992 had decided to devote themselves entirely to pleasuring small men from Bromley.

In 1982 a dispute over the ownership of some islands in the South Pacific was peacefully resolved in a Buenos Aires steakhouse with neither side pressing its claim on the grounds that the islands would shortly be rendered uninhabitable by the rapid advance of global freezing.

In 2008 an initiative from the much-loved 'investment' banks saw them volunteer to stop all their tax avoidance schemes, to put a firm and low ceiling on their own pay and bonuses, not to seek taxpayer refunds for their own failed bets and to agree a charter of their ethical obligations. This they signed in the blood of a unicorn, now once again the most populous equine on the planet.

In 1998 Martin McGuinness, former leader of the terrorist Provisional IRA, was appointed minister in charge of children's education in Northern Ireland.

In 2017 The Islamic Society for the Tolerance of Other

---

* Readers may care to spot the only one that did. Answer on page 120.

Points of View decided by a large majority that other religions had a lot to be said for them. A spokesman for the
Wahhabi Congress in Riyadh said he and his colleagues had
'laid it on a bit thick' lately and were now happy to welcome
other religions, their female adherents in particular, to join
them in paradise.

In 2012 a law was passed by the World Government that
legalised polygamy. However, its criteria were so strict that it
transpired that the only man legally entitled to sixteen wives
was found to be a 145-year-old moustachioed ex-draper's
assistant born in a Bromley china shop.

JEROME K. JEROME

still can't get to the point, even on an 18-30 holiday

When Mrs Drudge brought in the chops and porter and gooseberry tart for supper, she came across a lively debate while we were packing. Harris declared that he should be shaving off his moustaches.

'It's a crying shame,' he said, 'but I fear to give the "wrong signal".'

'Well,' George returned, 'I for one intend to wear the colours of my livery company in the ribbon of my boater.'

Harris said that his great uncle Wilberforce in his younger day had gone on a bicycling tour of the Crimea with a couple of other fellows and one night the three were compelled to share a single bunk in the attic of the local harbour master . . .

However, the presence of Mrs Drudge enforced a rare discretion upon Harris and spared us the remainder of this reminiscence.

Then we flew to Dubrovnik, transferred to our villa, unpacked and went to a club. A man clad only in a loincloth acted as the gatekeeper.

George said the fellow reminded him of something that once happened to his aunt in the Italian Alps. It was this lady's practice when travelling to take a supply of cambric handkerchiefs for distribution among the poor. On one occasion, suffering from hay fever, she was accosted in the street by . . .

Sadly the volume of the music that now assailed us prevented us from hearing the conclusion of this amusing tale. We appeared to be in a species of repository, though instead of storing furniture it seemed to be the half-clad human form that it was warehousing. Harris said it reminded him of the Whitsun weekend mannequin display in the window of Marshal and Snelgrove.

Some hours later we found ourselves watching a display of lubricious excess. The fellow behind George asked him to remove his boater as it was in his line of sight. George said the show brought to mind the experience of an old school friend who had once worked as a lifeguard in a nudist colony near Frinton-on-Sea. We got back to our digs in Dubrovnik at eight the next morning.

We did this every day for a week, then flew back to London and took a taxi to our lodgings. There was a welcome rattle on the stairs as Mrs Drudge staggered in with a shepherd's pie, a jug of ale and a rhubarb turnover.

'What was it like?' enquired the good lady.

'Well,' replied Harris. 'It reminded me of a holiday my uncle once took . . .'

HENRY FIELDING

made Tom Jones spend weeks in taverns – but not a modern one

Mr Jones having been absent from our tale yet awhile, the reader may wonder what befell the young gentleman when we left him upon the threshold of a Greenspring Health restaurant beside the thoroughfare of Lincoln's Inn. Let us then rejoin our young hero as he hungers for his midday victualling . . .

Jones threw down his tricorn and sword upon the nearest table and addressed a wench whose uniform concealed the twin joys of womanhood beneath an apron of the coarsest fustian.

'Don't bother me with bills of fare, woman, bring me of the landlord's plenty,' Jones commanded her. 'And a hogshead of ale to wash it down.'

'Not a problem,' said the wench. 'One dish of the day.'

As he waited, Jones propped his boots, muddied from six days in the saddle, upon a convenient table and lit his pipe. He smiled as he envisaged a leg of mutton, roasted fowl – and kidney pudding with a gross of oysters to begin.

In her due hour, the serving wench returned with a paper plate. Its contents were green, exiguous and unfamiliar to our hero, who nevertheless contained his disappointment with the largeness of humour that enabled his acquaintance – and perchance, we dare to hope, the reader also – to overlook his giddiness, his flatulence and his satyriasis.

'Zounds, but this is a monumental jest,' said he, slapping his breeches. 'You bring the garnish, but retain the dish. Like dear Sophia when she shows a glimpse of petticoat but conceals the joys beyond.'

'It's called a quinoa salad,' said the wench.

'Quinoa? What Popish nonsense is that?' said Jones. 'You force my hand, you impudent girl.'

So saying, he took her by the waist, bent her over his knee and administered a spanking such as old Thwackum had once imprinted on his own youthful person.

'Now then,' he roared. 'Bring me a basin of hot tripe with caper sauce, if you please. And tell the pretty maiden in the corner to come and join me this instant. I shall give her money enough to buy a skirt that's long enough to cover the limbs that she displays for my delight.'

But at that moment Jones's ardour and his outer clothing were doused by a downpour of water from a source concealed above his head.

'It's your pipe,' said a sickly-looking man with a beard. 'It's set off the sprinklers.'

WILLIAM BLAKE

turns travel agent, with one song of
Innocence *and one of* Experience

―――――――◄○►―――――――

At the Villa Soleil
You'll be happy all day.
It's just by the sea
And there's biscuits for tea.
It's perfect for Gran,
You can all get a tan.
And the food is delish,
Local salads and fish.

It's perfect for tots,
It can offer them lots.
There's tennis nearby,
Not a cloud in the sky.
You just ring for a maid
And find your bed's made
We all shout hooray
For the Villa Soleil.

**

Villa, villa, in the night,
Tacked on to a building site.
What bacterial grill or fry
Did cause that awful dysentery?

What mendacious hack or fool
Photoshopped a swimming pool?
What has caused the smell of feet
To overpower the master suite?

Who the plumber? Who the cook?
Who designed this squalid nook?
And did he smile his work to see?
Did he who made Toxteth make thee?

Villa, villa in the night
Deprived of any natural light
How could you have failed to say
You backed on to a motorway?

DANIEL DEFOE

cast Robinson Crusoe away on Ibiza, it turns out

———————◄○►———————

In my twenty-sixth year of solitude it happen'd one day about noon as I was procuring small fishes from my boat that an unseen Providence caus'd a mighty squall that drove my craft to the southernmost point of the island that in all my years I had feared to visit; where it founder'd upon some sharp rocks and I was wash'd upon the foreshore. I contriv'd to take with me only a fowling piece wrapp'd in cloth, some gunpowder and gold coins. It was now the middle of the night, yet a violent throbbing sound affrighted my imagination till I was terrify'd to the last degree. Nearing the pandemonium I took my spyglass; and from my point of lowly vantage in the sand I saw such a sight as surely neither God nor Providence had yet vouchsaf'd to human eye.

Thousand upon thousand of half-naked savages were leaping up and down in a ritual of frenzy that I conjectur'd was but a preparation for the killing and eating of some poor wretch among them. I had thought a Scotch man known to the savages by the name McKay had been their victim as he was push'd uncloth'd upon a wooden scaffold; though here he was not eat as I had thought but performed an act of conjugal lewdness upon his wife while the throng clapp'd hands about them.

One savage then crept off in search of water from a spring

whereon I surprised the fellow with a blow to the head from my fowling piece. On his recovering his wits I took him with me to where my boat, some what battered but still seaworthy, now lay upon the sand. At dawn with a following wind we made landfall at my palisade upon the north side of the island where I instructed the savage in the holy scriptures and in the making of goat broth. Four years passed in this way and I may say that never had a master a more faithful and devoted servant than this pagan that I rescu'd from the mouth of damnation.

A SHOT RANG OUT

MARCEL PROUST

has a crack at starting off a thriller

A shot – or rather memory of the sound made by the tapping of a hammer on the iron wheel of a locomotive of the seaside train as it stopped for a moment among the hawthorn hedges and the lilacs of a village in Normandy – was embodied in the hand-held automatic as the striker was released from tension by the action of the trigger and driven into the rear end of the cartridge, causing the ejection of the bullet from the barrel and the empty casing from the breech, while a trace of cordite lingered like the smell of my grandmother's fresh baked bread on Sunday morning before Mass, and the sensation of the trembling recoil on my skin recalled my mother's transient goodnight kiss; so that what had started as an act of violence, offered in the shallow flux of present time, devoid of memory and its handmaid, the imagination, became with the reverberation of the sound about the station concourse an unexpected gateway into permanence, where, like the church bells that signalled the approach of old Françoise with a pail of fresh milk from the village dairy, the echo of the brief explosion reverberated in the gulf of time past, and, sedulously manipulated by the violent hands of the present as the termination of a human life, became in

the patient clasp of involuntary memory, the means by which
the moment was neither lost nor permanent, but memorialised
as that in which a shot rang, with whatsoever reper-
cussions, out.

EDGAR ALLAN POE

does a murder mystery to the metre of The Raven

———————◆————————

I met her at a drunken ceilidh where the fiddlers fiddled gaily
And I'd drunk a fairish skinful of a curious forgotten brew.
I was dancing, madly bopping, suddenly there came a hissing
As of someone loudly kissing, kissing till her lips went blue –
      Just a slapper, nothing new.

This was all in deep December, maybe it was in November;
Anyway I can't remember how I got off with Lenore.
In the car park fiercely snogging, all at once I heard some
  jogging
As of someone wildly dogging, dogging by my Escort door.
      I forced my bird down on the floor.

She's engaged to dimwit Eddy, he prevents us going steady;
Says Lenore's a right posh item, just the kind to make a wife.
'Len,' I says, 'I move a motion. Brew me up a poison potion.
Eddy won't have any notion – notion of what took his life.
      If that fails, I'll use a knife.'

Wednesday night and Eddy bought it, spark out stiff, well
  who'd have thought it?
Len and I were laughing madly as we buried him beneath the
  floor.

She was chortling, nearly singing when there came a sudden
dinging
As of someone fiercely ringing, ringing on the old front door.
Now who on earth can that be for?

Four policemen slowly plodding, give the drains a good old
rodding.
Finding nothing, say they're sorry and they really should
have known.
As they're leaving, Lenny's sleeping, from the floor there
comes a beeping
Like a Nokia fiercely bleeping, bleeping out the old ring tone.
We've buried Eddy with his
phone.

Mr Plod had gathered the suspects together in the long room at Malory Towers.

'What we have here,' he said, 'is a gang killing. For some weeks the Secret Seven have been crossing the Famous Five postcode. This morning I discovered Mr Milko the Milkman had been run over by the train driver, Mr Train Driver.'

'Do you think that's his real name?' said Gobbo, the Goblin.

'Yes, I do,' nodded Noddy. He looked down at his feet where a dog, his friend Mr Bumpy Dog, had just bumped into him.

'Golly,' said Golly.

Big Ears sat down in the wishing chair. 'I wish I could lay my hands on the villain,' he said.

'Careful what you wish for,' said the Naughtiest Girl in the School.

'We need more evidence,' said Julian, sensibly.

'And what's your name, sonny?' said Mr Plod. 'Mr Sensible?'

'No. Julian.'

'And what sort of a name is that?' said Mr Plod.

'Forget it,' said Dick. 'I vote we do a DNA test on Mr Milko.'

'Couldn't we just have a picnic?' said Anne. 'I'll wash up.'

At that moment a man with a beret came through the door of Malory Towers. 'Bonjour,' he said in a funny voice. 'I have listened to what you say. And the murderer is clear. Mr Milko was pushed on to ze train track by a small animal. My friends, we are looking for a little dog who bump into people. Do you know such a person?'

The Famous Five looked blankly at the Secret Seven then back at the man with the moustache.

'And what do you think this Murderer might be called?' said Julian.

'You tell me,' said the Foreigner.

'Shut it, garlic breath,' said Mr Plod. 'You're nicked. Come with me.'

'What for?' said the Foreigner.

'For being foreign,' said Mr Plod.

'Jolly good,' said Anne. 'I hope he gets lashings of time inside.'

The body of Sir Hector Transome had been laid out in the library for Gertrude's inspection. The richest landowner in Warwickshire appeared to have been garrotted with the family jewels before being drowned in the mill race. The entire domestic staff was gathered in the twilight, their faces rapt.

Gertrude, however, found herself engrossed by the collection of Unitarian tracts on the library shelves. There was a complete set of Wesleyan hymns and almost all of Hegel and Spinoza. But why did no one these days read Feuerbach's seminal *Gedanken über Tod und Unsterblichkeit*?

'Pardon, Miss.'

Gertrude found her reverie interrupted by P. C. Bede from Nuneaton. 'Was it Lady Transome who done it? They was unhappily married you see.'

'Marriage is a state of higher duties,' replied Gertrude. 'I never thought of it as mere personal ease, when I wed a man fifty years my senior, incontinent, avaricious and incapable of the most perfunctory marital kindness.'

'Indeed,' said young Will Lawless, the tousle-headed adventurer who was Sir Hector's illegitimate son. 'But surely enlightened people can make arrangements beyond the constraints of society.'

The impudent young man appeared to have a twitch in his

eyelid, Gertrude remarked; unless . . . he was winking at her. No wonder, she thought with a shudder, that the village slatterns referred to him as the Divine Will.

'The solution you all crave is not easily dispensed,' Gertrude declared, surveying the row of credulous domestics. 'This library embodies mankind's futile search for a key to all mysteries. The jewels about Sir Hector's throat are the single pearls of wisdom that he gathered before drowning in the mill race of time. The miscreant you search is not among the humble people gathered here tonight. No parlour maid, or groom, no cook or housekeeper, no underfootman or even head footman could have wrought such an infernal deed.'

'You mean,' said Will, 'it is the work of the Supreme Power.'

'Yes, indeed,' cried Gertrude. 'The Butler did it.'

Virginia Woolf

once tried a crime story. Only once, though . . .

Cordelia Galloway was pruning roses in the walled garden at Tillingfold, distracted by the sensation of their perfume, their scent, their aroma.

'Call for you, Mrs G,' said Walsh, the odd-job man. 'Milton Keynes uniform branch.'

Mrs Galloway put her fingers to her temples. With Maynard Keynes she was familiar, but who was this Milton who so opportuned her by the electric telephone? As for the 'uniform branch', there could be no such thing. Every branch was particular, as G. E. Moore had established, unique in its own quiddity; none could therefore be 'uniform'.

'They're sending a car,' said Walsh. 'Young woman's been murdered.'

Cordelia was by way of being terrified of automobiles, unless they were driven by her own chauffeur, Billingham. On the back seat, she thought of how the variety and noise of the world closed down to a moment of silence, to a core of selfhood. She gazed through the glass at a vulgar settlement, a city, she supposed – a town.

At the police station, Cordelia met an officer whose bulging eyes gave him something of the toad.

'Inspector Ness,' he said, holding out his labourer's hand. 'But the lads just call me Ness.'

'Cordelia Galloway,' she returned. 'Private investigator from Russell Square.'

'Ah yes,' said Ness. 'The famous Bloomsbury Snoop.'

'I also write books. My last was published in instalments.'

'A serial thriller?' The coarse man chuckled.

'I have yet to hear *The Weeks* so described,' said Cordelia.

In the morgue Ness showed her the body of a young woman. Cordelia noted what appeared to be a mariner's tattoo above the coccyx.

'But, Ness,' she exclaimed, 'she's a common little tart!'

'She was,' said Ness, 'but she changed her ways. She was truly sorry.'

Cordelia took one last look at the body. 'You are quite right,' she declared. 'This girl was not murdered. She drowned in a stream of conscience, Ness.'

Dex Lewicki had been on secondment to the firm only six months, but already he'd seen too much. A shoplifting in Cowes. A parking violation in Seaview. But this was something else. This one smelled to high heaven.

'Right,' he said to Marion, the secretary. 'I want the reports from the CIA and your British equivalent of the FBI. What is it – M Fifteen?'

'Bear with me,' said Marion. 'M Fifteen? Well . . . There are two miles of slow moving traffic between Junction 12, Freshwater and Junction 13, Sandown. Or do you mean MI5?'

Lewicki fired up a Kool. 'What we got here, Marion, is corruption, top down. The Mayor of Ventnor's trying to pin the rap on the chair of the justices in Shanklin, but he's running for Boro' surveyor of Bembridge. We gotta nail this guy before he crosses the state line into Hampsheer.'

Marion giggled. 'Sounds like a job for the Sweeney. You know, Sweeney Todd, the—'

'Yeah, the Sondheim thing. I caught it last year at the Met.'

'No. Not the Met,' said Marion. 'They're the uniform branch.'

'Whatever,' said Dex. 'Now this Town Clerk of Freshwater guy. How's his rap sheet read? Misdemeanours? Felonies? Give me the whole nine yards.'

Marion looked at her screen. 'Bear with me. Yes, here we are. He has had an ASBO once.'

'Asbo? Yeah, I knew an Asbo once. Polish guy. DA in DC. Feds nailed his ass on a bum rap.'

'I don't think it's him,' said Marion. 'An ASBO's a punishment.'

Dex's eyes lit up. 'Our man is a felon? What he do?'

Marion peered at the screen. 'Morris dancing at Bembridge. Without a licence.'

SPORTS AND PASTIMES

RABBIE BURNS

turns his gaze for once on something very English: *Wimbledon.*

First ae caper syne anither gang the weans a silver tassie
Gie a skelp a gude swats the heed o' peely-wally lassie
Wee white kiltie shows her breeks, aye guiden grunt
Wi chiels that winna ding – fae thrifty Dougal, worth a punt.

Ye bonnie banks and backhand braes
Ye hawk-eye ganga kennin wrang
So gi's a neep and cantie mair
Srathspey your weans and wait yer hurry
Behold, yon Lochinvar is Andy Murray!

Wee sleekit cowrin' tim'rous Tim . . .
Wi' sonsie face, a spindle shank
The dreich that Cowdenbeath, Kilmarnock nil
Guid kennin gang thegither
Loathsome brae o' Henman Hill.

Aye . . . Gie's pint o' whisky, pint o' wine,
Nae pint o' bairnswee Pimms.
Tim's made a halesome parritch o' the smash,
The histie wuzzock's overheeds gang aft agley.
It wasnae Scotia's pride as donned guid kennin white
For ance: fareweel – and tak' the lowroad, Anglish shite!

THOMAS HARDY

is sent to cover the big match

———————◄○►———————

A traveller across that windy heath would have seen Wimborne Minster start the game well with a brace of neatly taken goals by the poacher, Boldwood, back from a loan spell with Charminster. The return of the native did not last long, however, as when celebrating his second, he slipped on ground made treacherous by a leaking gutter from the roof of the main stand and broke his back.

On the stroke of half-time, Farfrae, the new boy from Ayr, was penalised for handball, though replays clearly showed that the ball had not touched him. Egdon scored from the spot and the Minsters' lead was halved at the break.

While the teams were off, heavy snow fell and the gale-force wind, which had been in Wimborne's face for the first forty-five minutes, turned round to confront them with its bitter fury once again.

Henchard, the left-back, did not return to the field of play after the interval, when he discovered that his wife had been delivered of stillborn twins. Durbeville, Wimborne's close-season signing from Auxerre, was ruled ineligible when the Channel packet was delayed and his registration papers were accidentally delivered to the wrong address. To make matters worse for the Blues, Fawley, the other substitute, was found hanged in the team coach.

Reduced to nine men, Wimborne Minster battled bravely against the elements till the sixtieth minute, when Winterbourne, a tireless labourer in the middle of the park, felt his Achilles tendon snap. Troy scored a tap-in equaliser for the visitors in the eightieth minute.

In the pitiless rain, Wimborne held out till deep into stoppage time, when Everdene, on for the fatally injured Boldwood, sliced the ball into the roof of her own net from thirty yards. The President of the FA had, in the Aeschylean manner, finished his sport with Wimborne Minster.

TED HUGHES

*on the detention at an airport of
José Mourinho's Yorkshire terrier*

His eyes reflect the bed of lakes,
The sodden moors where
Stone walls endure his running and
A skyline bends to the gravity of loss.

His coat is an anchorite's thistle shirt,
His beard the tangle of the thief
Bound for van Diemen's land. His
Squat jaw would tear the head from a pullet.

Above the iron helmet of his skull
He wears the topknot bow, Plantagenet
Red, seeped in the war blood drained
From turf at Stamford Bridge.

To him in his wicker basket, there are
No borders and no quarantine.
On the drum of his caged ear resounds the
Screech of hung rabbits in his teeth.

All night in Departures, Terminal Two,
Through the crazed yapping of his tongue,
The long horizons reel.

W. B. YEATS

reports on the 2006 Ryder Cup at Kildare

———————◄○►———————

The restless multitude is pressed where
The wild falcon and the linnet wing
By Kildare's foam-thrashed sea:
More albatross than eagle, more
Eagle than birdie, less birdie than halved in par
In the afternoon four-balls
With Woods and Love.

Love and innocence is born in Seven Woods
At Sligo in the spring,
Though a five-wood's all that's needed with the wind
    behind.
I think now of Kiltartan's sons whose names
The English Belfry tolled in widening gyres,
The Irish soldiery gone beneath the mire:
Paul McGinley, Padraig Harrington, a tattered stick
Of Dublin rock upon the threatening fifth;
Christy O'Connor Senior, sixty years the pro at Lissadell,
Taken by the fairy as a child and shown the interlocking
    grip,
More overlapping than interlocking,
A public smiling man whose high slice
Loosed left-handed Eamonn Darcy on the world.

And in the final singles, as the sun falls behind
The lakeside tower, I watch him
Take the hickory stick. His limbs dance to a frenzied
    drum,
His unsure grip bespoke
By Lady Gregory's own assiduous putting stroke
Perfected on the borrowing lawns at Coole.

An old man is a paltry thing who hides his head
And cannot watch the white orb roll towards the cup.
So may it be that when I am long stymied
And gone beneath the divot
Under bare Ben Hogan's Head,
You may always pierce the veil and dream
Of Christy O'Connor Junior's soaring three-iron
To the gull-tormented eighteenth green.

SEAMUS HEANEY

loved his native land, which was not *the Home Counties*

My father taught me what his uncle once showed him:
To strike the safety match away from me.
The diphthong of emery and phosphorus was
The flare of Surrey dialects. I tossed the wooden 'l'
Into the tongueless babel of charcoal.

By God, the old man could handle a Volvo.
He drove at sixty on the old A3,
His eye fixed on Hog's Back, where
Norman raiders glimpsed the upland, their
Rapine footprint dripping from Virginia Water.

In the scullery, my mother plunging raw hands
In white ceramic, pulled up gold. Egg yolks
Dripped through the webbing of her fingers.
Legs planted like a pair of cricket bats,
She drew the wisdom of the Sussex Downs
Into the alchemy of quiche lorraine.

The sausages spat protest at the flame, like
Cranmer burned by Catholics at the stake.
The T-bone wore a charred lattice of sectarian
Divide. My aunt appeared at last after a
Century, when dug out from the bog.

To the longboat roar of Guildford bypass, we
Drank all night, our kinship hammered out
On Beaujolais, discovering at dawn
The reinsurance market had gone belly-up;
And with it, all my father's cash at Lloyd's.

GERARD MANLEY HOPKINS

decides to clean his car, a Vauxhall

—◆◇◆—

I washed this morning Sunday morning's office, oblation,
Obligation – purifying man's four-door estate.
Garbed in chasuble, proof against
Watersplash, dash from bucket brim,
Down damp door sills and air-filled tyres, tireless
In black, the soap sings to the sheen of the chamois and shower –
Carburettor, biretta, camshaft, big end
Oil pump, plump purple, vermilion, where the Lord
Moves in motor ways, hatchback and patch, hard-
    shouldering me
Windscreen-wiped, wheel-wetted wagon of rapture.

Inside I brushed footwell and mock-leather trim,
Disconnected the sat-nav, no need of direction
Save only His who showed men the true way, the one-way,
Led free to lead-free, the fuel of heart's heat.

But sheer suds and power-polish palm work make hubcaps
    gleam
And the fire that shines panel of glory with – ah, labourful,
    luminous love,
My roadster, redeemer – oh, my Cavalier!

RAYMOND CHANDLER

began his writing life as a poet – perhaps
with a Shakespearean sonnet

Should I compare you to a Chevrolet?
No, you pack more power beneath the hood;
The tailback on Sunset bars my way,
The lousy price of gas can spoil the mood.
Sometimes the fender gets stove in
When a guy rear-ends you as you hit the brake.
Every automobile has its fill of rovin',
Sold on to some young hustler on the make.

But your upholstery will never dim,
Your speed and comfort always set to thrill;
No Junkyard Joe can crush your bodywork to him
No rust will touch your hub or subframe sill.
   So long as men can lift the dipswitch to full beam,
    The headlamps of your eyes will make them dream.

JOHN KEATS

once wrote a sonnet to a non-poetic subject, a traffic jam

———————◄○►———————

When I have fears that I may not arrive
Before my friends have cleared their groaning plates
Before I've climbed out of my Renault Five
Or even had the chance to greet my mates;
When I behold upon the gridlocked street
The blushing tail lights of the moonlit queue
And think that I may never get to eat
The dew-fresh salad or the monkfish stew;
And when I feel, my neighbour for tonight,
That I may never see your laughing eyes,
As I sit for ever at the amber light
Of non-reflective glass – then at the rise
Of Hanger Lane I stall alone and think:
Don't let the bastards finish all the drink.

IAN FLEMING

finds an everyday job for his retired hero

Bond stilled the roar of the Amherst-Villiers supercharger and stopped the Bentley at the end of the suburban cul-de-sac. He thought how much he loathed the new company crest on the door: 'The Service. Plumbing and Heating Engineers. 24 Hours. Emergency'.

He spotted a parking place between a Renault Twingo and a Hyundai Pony. He eased the Bentley into it masterfully and took his tool bag from the boot. The pink docket Tracy had given him at the office said: 'Customer's Name: Mrs Sappho Crumpet.' Bond's mouth tightened into a cruel line. He enjoyed a challenge.

Mrs Crumpet let him into the kitchen. She had a platinum perm and a badly blocked sink.

'I'm going to have to rod your drains,' said Bond.

'Go on, then,' said Mrs Crumpet.

Bond took out his Vesper 416 power hose with the 2000-watt cold fusion battery. For perhaps ten minutes he used it cruelly.

'No dice,' said Bond eventually. 'Can you show me the inspection hatch?'

Mrs Crumpet took him outside. Between the potting shed and a garden gnome was what Bond wanted: an innocent-looking iron rectangle let into the crazy paving. In an instant, Bond was deep beneath the foundations, crawling through the watery underworld. He estimated he was directly under the kitchen sink when he saw something odd. It was a recording device with the telltale label: Property of SPECTRE.

I might have known, thought Bond. Surbiton Plumbing Electrical Carpentry Tiling and Roofing Experts – the Firm's deadliest rival.

'We meet again, Mr Bond,' said a voice behind him.

It was Ernie Coldfinger, SPECTRE's master of leaks.

'Indeed,' said Bond. 'I expected to find a rat in a sewer.'

Bond never liked having to kill people, but it was part of his job. He pulled out his Walton PPK adjustable spanner and did what was necessary, coldly, without remorse. That would teach SPECTRE to steal the Service's clients, he thought, as he watched the corpse float away.

'Cup of tea, Mr Bond?' said Sappho Crumpet, back in the kitchen.

'No thanks,' said Bond. 'Tea's for old maids. Let me have a cocktail of Wolfschmidt vodka, Dom Perignon '55 and a dozen Benzedrine.'

'Coming right up,' said Miss Crumpet.

'Well, something is, Sappho,' said Bond.

ENTER STAGE RIGHT

TERENCE RATTIGAN
tried the gritty new drama – only once, in French With Tears

———————◦———————

A squat in the port area of Marseille. Monsieur, the landlord, and various young English exchange guests are finishing breakfast.

HUGO: Anyone for tennis?

MONSIEUR: What is the point of tennis? It is the definition of *ennui*. The pit of man's despair.

SALLY: It's jolly good exercise, Monsieur.

MONSIEUR: Get back on the street, *salope*. Like Madame my wife. That is her exercise.

HUGO: Last time I played tennis I was—

MONSIEUR: Say it in French. You are 'ere to learn.

HUGO: Golly, all right. La dernière fois, j'étais tout autour du magasin.

MONSIEUR: What does he say?

SALLY: He means last time he played he was all over the shop.

HUGO: I say, Monsieur, can I lend you my translation of John Buchan? It's really awfully good.

MONSIEUR: No, I read only the *Etoile du Matin*. The Communist paper, how you call it, *The Morning Star*.

SALLY: Morning Star? I saw him run at Goodwood last year. A lovely frisky bay with a black tail.

MONSIEUR: I tell you a black tale, Mademoiselle. My son is in prison. He is awaiting trial for stealing a postal order.

HUGO: What awfully bad luck. But I'm training to be a barrister myself and I'd love to represent the poor boy.

MONSIEUR: It does not look good for him. He was selling drugs to the gang leader at the dock to pay for the abortion of his girlfriend. His house was condemned because of the rats and he needed money for medicine for his venereal disease.

HUGO: Gosh, that's what we call a real *drame d'évier de cuisine*.

SALLY: He means a kitchen-sink drama, Monsieur.

MONSIEUR: Also the boy 'ave twelve previous conviction for soliciting, arson and 'ouse breaking.

HUGO: The boy is plainly innocent. I accept the brief.

MONSIEUR: No, you fool. He is guilty. I am his pimp. 'Ere is the money. Now let's all get *totalement pissés commes des tritons*. [*Pop*] *Salut*!

HUGO: What's he say, Sally?

SALLY: Never mind, Hugo.

TOM STOPPARD

writes an episode of The Archers

The public bar of the Bull. At the bar are Clarrie Grundy, Edvard Munch, Ruth Archer and Ludwig Wittgenstein, who has come for a job as cellarman. Behind the bar are Sid Perks and his wife Jolene. Other regulars sit about the room.

SID: Ludwig, meet my wife Jolene Perks.

WITTGENSTEIN: Mmm. Is she one of ze perks of ze job?

SID: No. But she's got two of the nobs of the Perks.

WITTGENSTEIN: I had not known zat in philosophy you were such a dualist.

RUTH ARCHER: Whoah no, Ludwig, man. Don't go puttin' Descartes before the 'orse.

IAN CRAIG: Noy then, noy then. Just because I'm a gay Olsterman doesn't mean I can't be screamingly normal.

EDVARD MUNCH: Thank you, Ian. I am a Norwegian expressionist. I would like to paint your Scream.

WITTGENSTEIN: A scream? May I refer you to my Tractatus Logico-Philosophicus.

EDDIE GRUNDY: I don't know about your tractatus, but Oi got a Massey Ferguson.

JOLENE: A massive what?

EDDIE GRUNDY: Ferguson.

CLARRIE: Oh, Eddie!

Enter Nigel Pargeter

NIGEL: Did the artist chappy say his name was Munch? My pater used to say that where there's Munch there's Braque.

Enter Georges Braque.

BRAQUE: Mr Perks, I zink you find ze answer in Schopenhauer.

JACK WOLLEY: Oh yes, Peggy. Ev'ry Wednesday five o'clock we have a shoppin' hour at Grey Gables. Very popular with the ladies.

Enter Alistair, the vet.

ALISTAIR: Half of Shires, please, Sid. I've spent all morning trying to neuter Schrödinger's Cat. Couldn't tell if he was dead or alive by the end. Possibly both at once.

WITTGENSTEIN: I sink you should try ze vasectomy. A small part of ze *vas deferens* is excised and ze two loose ends tied off.

BRIAN ALDRIDGE: Oh yes, Jennie insisted I have that op once. But I can't say it made a vas' difference to me . . . Or Siobhan!

Enter Rob Titchener

ROB (darkly): Anyone seen Helen?

LINDA SNELL: She was hiding in my Resurgam Garden.

TONY ARCHER: What do you want Helen for anyway, Titch?

WITTGENSTEIN: Careful, Tony! Whereof one cannot speak, thereof –

Enter Walter Gabriel.

WALTER GABRIEL (for it is he): Hello me old beauty, me old darling!

WITTGENSTEIN: Walter! I thought you were dead!

WALTER GABRIEL: No more than that cat you was on about. How's the old Tractatus?

WITTGENSTEIN: Mustn't grumble, Walter. Bert Fry's fixed her up a treat.

WALTER GABRIEL: Good show. I don't know why we are here, Ludwig, but I'm pretty sure that it is not in order to enjoy ourselves!

Dum, di dum, di dum, di dum, dum, di dum, di dum, dum . . .

SOPHOCLES

never dramatised really minor *disasters — until now*

————————◄○►————————

CHORUS
Oh what unhappy youth approaches
Tearing at his clothes in grief?
Who turns his face to heaven
Where the implacable Fates
Prepare his grievous end?
He strikes first this side with
His hand and then the left
As one whose body burns
Within a covering of fire.

OEDIPUS
I have lost the keys to this my home.
I curse the day that first my
Father let me have a spare.
Now all the wrath of Heaven
Awaits my entry to this hearth.
Begone, foul townsmen!
Mock not my tears' libation
At the family step! Must now
I wake the terror of the monstrous
Dog by ringing at the bell?
What awful grief my murderous

Mother now portends with
Evil omens where the gods
Demand a sacrifice of blood.
Oh heavy load that I should so
Disgrace this sacred house.
What further woe, what shame
Can I unleash within these
Cursed doors? Surely now
This is my fated end at last.

CHORUS
Be not so sure, young man.
The worst is yet to come if
We can say this is the worst.
Strike not at the crossroads.
Take not the widow of your king.
Best turn away to Corinth,
While your parents are annoyed.
Above all, young man, don't make
Yourself a whipping boy for Freud.

TENNESSE WILLIAMS

is at home in the deep south . . . of England

PENELOPE: Oh, baby, I glimpsed you from the fire escape. Did you hear the jazz band playing in the street? Did you hear them? Did you take the streetcar like Ah told you?

GERALD: No. Briggs dropped me off.

PENELOPE: Ah do believe a lady is allowed a cocktail at this hour. Some bourbon over ice is what Ah take.

GERALD: I could offer you a glass of Pimm's.

PENELOPE: It sounds . . . aromatic. All those herbs with brilliant colours, purple, midnight indigo . . . In the drink they carry all the swamp and festerin' o' Mississippi.

GERALD: I think it's made in Norfolk.

PENELOPE: Oh baby, you remember that summer with the houseboat on the Delta of the Ouse?

GERALD: The Norfolk Broads, you mean?

PENELOPE: The Norfolk broads are what came between us, baby. Those ladies from Thet-ford. And those belles from Swaff-ham.

She slumps down on a small stuffed stool.

GERALD: I was not the only one, Penelope.

PENELOPE: You referrin' to my gentlemen callers? Pour me another Pimm's, baby. I had mah admirers, it's true. But all I want . . . is you to make love to me now, Gerald. Am Ah not pretty enough? And what we gonna tell Big Daddy?

GERALD: You know I'm not a wrestling fan, Penelope. And you're drunk. I could tell by the way you sat down on that stool.

PENELOPE: And how'd I sit down, Mr Know-it-All Englishman?

GERALD: Like a . . . like a twat on a squat thin pouffe.

PENELOPE: Oh, baby, I welcome your kind words o' warnin'. All my life Ah have pretended to a blindness of dangers.

PLAYING TO THE CROWD

KARL OVE KNAUSGAARD

took his title, My Struggle, *from an earlier* Mein Kampf

———————◆———————

I had a phone call from Josef in the morning. 'Why don't you come to Wannsee for this thing at the weekend? It'll be fun.'

'Maybe,' I said. 'I was just going to hang out. And I won't be able to bring any beers. I haven't got any ID.'

I looked out of the window. The weather was grey. There was a building, some bricks, and a car.

'Reinhard's got some great ideas,' said Josef. 'Do you remember Albie Speer from the fifth year? He's coming.'

'My mum's moved north with her new boyfriend,' I said. 'I can't use her car any more.'

I'd met this girl called Eva in the seventh year. She had a stripy top and trainers. She wasn't really pretty like Marlene, but she was nice. I thought there was a chance if I could get some beers with my dad's credit card that I'd get to kiss her. What I really hoped was I'd get to first base with Eva without for once, just this once, please God, coming in my Lederhosen.

I went to the supermarket and put a bottle of salad cream and some margarine in my basket. Then I bought some tissues and some tinned peas. I looked at the smoked Wurst, but remembered I'd gone vegetarian. I went outside and it was cloudy. Next to the supermarket there was a car, and a building.

Back home I listened to some Wagner and played along, imagining I was the conductor. Then I read a book about this kid called Young Werther. He just wanted to be different from the other kids, but he could never really connect to anything much.

Josef rang again the next day about this Wannsee party. 'Otto's definitely coming,' he said. 'And do you remember that crazy guy Adolf Whatsit?'

'Eichmann? The one who stuck his dick in the beer bottle at Heinrich's birthday party?'

'Sure. Big Adsie. He's borrowed a tank, so you can have a lift.'

'Maybe. I was thinking of going into Russia, actually.'

'Russia? What for, man?'

'I think if I borrow my dad's car I can probably get some beers there.'

I looked out of the window and there was a building and a tree, and some bricks, and no car.

It was a shit weekend. I couldn't decide whether to go the Wannsee thing or invade Russia. I heated a tin of soup.

José went into the library to read a book, the professor followed, he was a very important and learned professor of intelligence, this was a highly significant activity, Javier took a cigar from the box on the table, intelligence could mean spying, that was the thing where you pretended to be someone else and had Significant exchanges, the professor was not listening, he was reading a book, it was Proust, José knew Proust had very long sentences with the architecture of a great cathedral with its stress equations and proportions in a golden harmony, but that's utter *cojones*, thought José, I know better, I was once a fellow at All Souls don't you know, he took a lighter for his cigar, there was no point in going to that trouble, he poured himself a drink, all you have to do is change your full stops and semi-colons into commas, the professor smiled at his guest, this is fun, thought José, here comes another clause, it's like the trucks on a goods train, chuff, chuff, went the professor, puff, puff, went José, the door opened, a mouse ran up the clock, José jumped over the moon . . .

DAN BROWN

visits the cash dispenser

---◂◦▸---

The world-renowned author stabbed his dagger-like debit card into the slot. 'Welcome to NatWest,' barked the blushing grey light of the screen to the forty-two-year-old man. He had only two thoughts.

NatWest is a perfect heptogram.

Scratching his aquiline head, frantically trying to remember a number, the sun came up at last and rained its orange beams on Dan Brown. 'What do you want to do?' asserted the blinking screen. His options were stark for Brown, more than ever now. 'Get Mini Statement'. 'Withdraw Cash'. 'Change PIN'. For what seemed an eternity, trying to remember his PIN, the screen mocked the famous writer.

Someone somewhere knows my four-figure PIN.

Whatever my PIN was once is still my PIN and in some remote safe someone somewhere still knows it.

In Paddington Station, an iconic railway terminal with a glass roof like the bastard offspring of a greenhouse and a railway station, a line of fellow travellers was waiting on Brown. Brown frowned down at his brown shoes and for the hundredth time that morning wondered what destiny may have in store for the Exeter, New Hampshire graduate.

The sandy-haired former plagiarism defendant felt his receding temples pounding in his guts. *Four figures. Four figures, you halfwit*, he almost found himself murmuring in Brown's ear, close at hand.

Tentatively his fingers pounded their remorseless melody upon the NatWest keyboard, numerically. He watched his fingers work with sallow eyes.

He typed in anything, literally anything, desperately. He didn't know what affect it may have.

The headquarters of the Royal Bank of Scotland resides in a hydraulically sealed ninety-eight-storey building guarded by hair-trigger sensitive nuclear firedogs at 4918, 274th Street in Manhattan, America, whose security protocol is known to only six elves whose tongues have been cut out for security by the Cyrenian Knights of Albania, the capital of Greece.

In an instant, the famous writer remembered their bleeding skin from barbed wire.

Of course. They must pass on the secret PIN. An unbroken chain whose links are not forged (not in that sense).

9 . . . 8 . . . 7 . . . 6. His fingers pronounced the Sigma number. The Sigma number was almost impossible to fake, whereby the Liberace Sequence was quite easy to forge for prominent author Dan Brown.

The cash machine cleared its throat and breathed in with a rasping exhalation that seemed to shake its very belly. Then finally it expectorated wheezily up twenty-eight million dollars into the fingers pregnant with expectation of the forty-two-year-old man.

'Take your cash now please,' pleaded the mocking screen, no longer mocking.

It's like giving candy to a baby, it occurred to the universe-celebrated prose stylist.

It's like shelling eggs.

P. G. WODEHOUSE
writes the Diary of Sir Walter Raleigh

Having just returned from two years in the New World, where I had acquired a sackful of seed potatoes and a hundred weight of tobacco, I was surfacing from a restorative ten hours, when my varlet, Grieves, oozed into my tower with a disapproving cough.

'I found this item of attire outside the bedchamber last night, Sir Walter. I presumed you had attended an entertainment of a theatrical nature and inadvertently brought home the costume worn by the jester.'

'That item,' I replied, and I meant it to sting, 'is a velveteen pelisse, or cloak. I wore it on the Spanish main all summer. It drew many admiring glances from the ladies.'

'Perhaps they thought you were a matador, Sir Walter.'

'Dash it, Grieves, I shall wear it at court this evening when I go to introduce my potatoes to her Majesty.'

'As you wish, sir. The feculent tuber is not something I feel her majesty, conscious as she is of the royal figure, will be desirous of consuming.'

I pushed an anxious hand across the b. 'Perhaps. But I'm pretty sure she'll go for the tobacco. Everyone in the New World was smoking it.'

'It is somewhat difficult to envisage her majesty with a

branch of brier in her mouth emitting clouds of smoke, Sir Walter. I fear the royal bodyguard may fear she has inadvertently caught fire and take measures to douse her person.'

Well I saw what the fellow meant, of course, and it was a pensive W R who strolled beside her majesty at Hampton Court that evening. Between the parterres was a large and stagnant puddle at which she hesitated, letting I dare not wait upon . . . something about a cat. I heard a discreet cough at my shoulder and the next thing I knew I found the velveteen pelisse in my hand. Well, it was with me the work of an instant to lay it down and so secure a dry passage for the royal slipper.

When I asked Grieves to return the garment that night, an evasive expression appeared on the blighter's face. 'I fear, sir, that the cloak's unforeseen immersion has rendered it unwearable. I have . . . er disposed of it accordingly. It is the poet Shakespeare who—'

'No one's heard of this bally poet Shakespeare,' I said sharply.

'As you wish, Sir Walter. Will that be all for tonight?'

T. S. ELIOT

reflects that it might have come out better in limericks

―――――――◄○►―――――――

THE WASTE LAND

Said a Lloyd's clerk with mettlesome glands:
'To Margate – I'll lie on the sands.
The Renaissance and Dante,
Dardanelles and now – Shanti!
God, it's all come apart in my hands.'

ASH WEDNESDAY

The weight of the past makes me pine
For a language that's English, but mine.
No more hog's-head and Stilton,
And to prove I'm not Milton,
I'll compose with four beats to a line.

The Journey of the Magi

We were freezing, ripped off and forlorn,
As we travelled towards a false dawn;
But the truth of the stable
Showed my world was a fable;
Now I wish that I'd never been born.

The Love Song of J. Alfred Prufrock

I once missed the moment to be
Someone not on the periphery;
But my second-hand life
Was too dull for a wife:
Now the stairlift awaits only me.

Four Quartets

For an Anglican, time is too vast;
A rose or a vision can't last:
It's a moment in history,
Our grace and our mystery,
And the future is lost in the past.

JOHN OSBORNE

takes Jimmy Porter off his sweet stall to make a speech

Ladies and Gentlemen – or at least you think you are in your borrowed morning suits and marshmallow hats. I know your kind. Oh yes, you're trying to strangle the life out of my daughter. Alice. God knows how we managed to have a child. Her mother – or Attila as she's called by those who know her – managed to avoid having enough babies to run a Woolworth's pick 'n' mix before Alice stuck it out. Oh yes, she's got her mother's ruthlessness all right.

She may look like a jelly baby but believe me she's a toffee brittle you can break your molars on. That's called a metaphor. I read it in a posh weekly that was trying to make me feel stupid. I bet the writer had never worked on a sweet stall. And anyone who's never weighed out a bag of dolly mixture is suffering from a pretty bad case of virginity.

And here's the groom, young Peregrine. Don't be fooled, 'Perry', don't be lulled by all that softness when you're married. She's a Gulag commandant, my daughter. She's a Shankhill Road butcher. Any feelings of being human that you have, she'll drain them out of you like a . . . like a . . . like an Eton boy sucking up a sherbet dip.

So you're a teacher are you, Peregrine? In a 'comprehensive'? But what can <u>you</u> comprehend? Do you fill their little heads with sentimental yarns of old Empire? What can you possibly know about <u>real</u> life? Ever run out of Maltesers on a Friday afternoon? Ever had to shoo a bluebottle from the liquorice twirls? I thought not. One day I'll wake you from your death-in-life complacency. Believe me, I've no public-school scruples about hitting comprehensive teachers.

So, Daddy and Mummy are from Wiltshire, are they? The family that put the Pewsey into Pusillanimous. I suppose my daughter is expecting? I'm surprised you're still alive to tell the tale. Normally after mating in our family the female consumes the male. Gobble. Gulp. One shudder and he's swallowed in the giant maw of all that . . . all that candy-coated, oh so considerate . . . kindness.

Ladies and Gentlemen . . . those of you still here. Raise your glass to the Bride and Groom, the Died in Gloom.

DOROTHY PARKER

is famous for saying witty things at Algonquin lunches,
but in fact she was mostly suicidal and wrote in verse

I pondered lonely as a cab
That's stalled on Tenth and Madison,
When all at once I felt a stab,
A pang that made me sad as one
Beneath the car, beside the trees,
Muttering and whining in the breeze.

Unending as the lamps that shine
And mark the end of gloomy day
And mock the failures that are mine
Along the length of all Broadway:
Ten thousands cocktails at a guess
Have washed me to this twilight mess.

The puddles of the sidewalk threw
Reflections of the ghastly night;
A poet could not but be blue
Confronted by this awful sight.
I moaned and groaned but never thought
What wealth to me this stuff had brought.

And often when in bed I've lain
In bitter, suicidal mood,
The lamps reflect my inner pain
In verses that are short and crude.
And then self-harm is my delight;
My husbands say it serves me right.

BETWEEN
THE SHEETS

JACKIE COLLINS

goes posh and literary, like a fourth Brontë

Cathy Earnswell lived in a to-die-for penthouse in Wutherley Hills. Her fabulously rich father owned *the* late-night place of choice in Micklethwaite. Cathy regarded her nude form in the mirror and marvelled at her ten grand's worth of boob job, teeth whitening and elocution lessons. 'I'm worth every last farthing,' she thought. Just then the incredible 210-pound Latino pool-boy called Studcliff sauntered in. His eyes were liquid black pools, his chiselled abs were exploding from his jerkin and he had way too much attitude for his menial job.

It was lust at first sight. Studcliff was a legendary swordsman who put seven sovereigns' worth of white powder a week up his cute little nose. Studcliff liked to wander on the bleak moors above Wutherley Hills where he had a weird nature thing. But Cathy, whose idea of the great outdoors was a Friday-night dogging, couldn't get enough of him.

Till one day she met mega-rich Edgar 'Eddie' Lintonio, who ran a top-of-the range, state-of-the-art business in Heptonstall. His father was a world-renowned neurosurgeon with acute business savvy, his mother was the heir to a string of luxury hotels and kid sister Isabella was the raunchiest chick this side of Hebden Bridge. She was already an action-movie mega-star and head of rocket science for All Europe. She had a brain the size of Ilkley Moor and an ass as pert as a Pontefract cake.

Then Cathy had a brainwave. She could marry Edgar Lintonio, suck up his millions and play the little wifey while still seeing Studcliff on the side for mind-blowing bouts of wildness between her silicone bust and his prodigious endowments in every superlative department.

She checked her diamond Rigatoni watch and narrowed her eyes to fierce slits. This'll make *Jane Eyre* look like a vicarage picnic she told herself, originally.

Unfortunately, that fall she got super-rare dengue fever and died. But Studcliff dug her up out of her grave for the kinkiest night of passion ever. She was literally in heaven.

◄○►

'Oh Thad,' purred Dolores, slipping off her beautiful new shoes and standing in a silken underskirt, 'you always seem to know what I'm thinking. It's as though you can read my mind.'

'I can,' said Thad. 'And by the way, I don't do that thing you're picturing. Not on a first date.'

'Mmm, Thad,' said Dolores when they had finished their love-making. 'Did the earth move for you?'

'Sure,' said Thad, frowning in furious concentration as he used his telekinetic powers to move the four-poster back into the bedroom from the rooftop where they lay.

'My sweetest Thad,' said Dolores, 'you have started a fire in my heart.'

'*What?*' said Thad. 'That was meant to be my old teacher's house. Pyrokinesis. Don't move, Dolores, I'm going to call 911.'

'Too late, my sweet,' said Dolores. 'A part of you is mine for ever. And you can't take it back.'

As she made for him with a giant machete, Thad ran out of the house. But a minute later he was back, shame-faced, at the front door.

'You know that thing, Dolores, that . . . part of me, that's, like, yours for ever. I discovered what it was and I'd . . . kind of like it back.'

But it was too late. Suddenly, Christina, the over-possessive station wagon, rolled up her headlights in anger and reversed vengefully over Thad, crushing his brains out on the driveway.

'Oh Thad, my dearest love,' cried Dolores.

But then . . . Oh, what the heck? thought Dolores. This bedroom stuff is for sissies. Give me a hobbling sledge-hammer and a bucket of pig's blood and I'll give you 'romance'!

The football game had been going ten minutes when Kev felt obliged to make an effort at conversation.

'Who's your mortgage with, Trev?'

'The Abbey National,' said Trev, wishing it sounded somehow less ecclesiastical, or at any rate more provincial.

'Fixed rate or variable?'

'Collar and cap, actually,' said Trev, blushing as he wondered if this suggested something on offer from a Soho *grisette*.

A burly man in a coloured nylon shirt with a number on its back squeezed in between them.

'Bob, Trev, Trev, Bob,' said Kev with a reluctant irony that seemed to hold out little hope for either.

'That new winger,' said Bob with an inclusive relish, ''e's a fuckin' genius.'

'Quite,' said Kev, leaving it tantalisingly ambiguous whether by 'quite' he meant definitely or moderately so.

'Hot dog?' said Trev at half time, shouldering his way to the stall where a young woman served boiled saveloys in cotton-wool buns.

'Fantastic tits,' said Trev, appreciatively looking up at

the vendeuse as she squeezed tomato sauce from a self-referentially shaped container.

'You bet,' said Kev, suddenly engorged at the thought of their . . . their . . . *binarity*. Two of them. Corr, thought Kev. Two! *Phwoarrr*.

'Don't get many of them to the pound,' said Trev appreciatively, but with a faint regret, as though he wished that the mammary to avoirdupois ratio had been a fraction more favourable.

The football pitch was greened with a verdigris of age and longing. In the matrix of the white rectangle the perspiring players moved in dazzling ellipses, now pausing for a plié or an arabesque more daring or ironic than the last, eliciting the hoarse commendation of their supporters.

'Wanker!' they cried. 'Send him off!' when one of the visitors tumbled like a stricken Giselle inside the white marquetry of the penalty 'box'.

'What route you take your kids to school?' said Kev.

For twenty minutes they discussed the school run, its cut-throughs, its anfractuosities, its triumphs and seasonal vagaries, in such a way that Kev felt obscurely proud to be both such a fecund breeder and so resourceful a navigator.

Bob passed him a plastic pint of lager and Kev inhaled its fizzy bouquet. He drank deep, and felt its chilly gas revive the dormant hot-dog onions in his gut. Recalling the elegant duality of the vendor's breasts, he belched with unambiguous relish.

'Cheers, Kev,' said Trev.

'Cheers, Trev,' said Kev.

The tense obbligato of 'Colonel Bogey' sounded in Trev's pocket and he fished out a vermilion Nokia.

'Did you remember the yoghurt?' It was his wife. 'Did you get the baby wipes? What time will you—'

'Sorry, love, terrible reception,' Trev said, squeezing the disconnect button with hesitant finality.

Kev, meanwhile, stared straight ahead, his eyes focussed on neither Rovers nor United, but on a midfield of ironic conjecture.

E. M. FORSTER

imagines a more liberal age in his posthumous Tea in Venice

————————◀◉▶————————

Aubrey Winsome had never liked the vaporetto; it reminded him of the steam engines that used to take him back to Bastards, his brutal private school in Surrey. And this morning it seemed especially tiresome as he found himself seated next to Archie Trader, who talked about his annual bonus from the private equity company that employed him.

But at that moment Aubrey saw someone who might be his special friend: Giancarlo Finocchio, the pagan gondolier he'd chanced across during last night's *ballo in maschera*. Giancarlo waved his left hand in greeting to Aubrey as with his right he pulled out his wooden pole from the lagoon. Aubrey smiled. Giancarlo was all rough edges and anachronisms, like a Quattrocento bike boy.

That afternoon in the Scuola San Rocco, as he stood rapt before the Tintorettos, Aubrey heard a polite little scream. It was Miss Honeywell, the English teacher, and the clasp on her handbag had tragically broken.

What happened next was like a bulletin from the world of panic and email. Miss Honeywell's mobile phone fell with a terrible tinkle to the marble floor. As Archie Trader went to help her, one of the great Tintorettos, unstable from many centuries of hanging, fell from its wall and crushed the mercantile man to death – killed by the art he had ignored.

Freed by this sudden death from social obligation, Aubrey sauntered back across the Piazza San Marco to where a special friend was waiting.

'Signore,' said Giancarlo, 'now I take you on my Ducati over rough roads. You meet my mother. Then we have . . . linguine for dinner? Is good?'

'Rath—er,' said Aubrey. 'Only connect, dear boy, only connect . . .'

JOHN LE CARRÉ
tries his hand at chick lit

Fiona had finally persuaded hunky George Smiley to book a mini-break, and next morning she received a printed post-card, second class. 'Come to the Mason's Arms, Railway Road, Beaconsfield at five o'clock. Ask for Mr White.'

Fiona screeched to a halt outside the hotel in her red Jilly Cooper Gti. The reception area smelled of Bovril and paraffin. She had hoped for a log fire and champagne. After a *sotto voce* exchange by telephone, the night manager gained clearance to show Fiona to a safe room on the first floor. The single bed had a candlewick counterpane, and through the net curtain she could see the exit *and* the entrance to the car park.

George returned from the bathroom down the landing and cleaned his spectacles on his tie, slowly, carefully, then replaced them on his nose.

'Did anyone see you come in?' he said.

'Only the night porter,' said Fiona. 'Now, come on, Mr Grumpy, get those braces off.'

'Were you followed?' said George. 'Do Brian's people know you're here?'

'Brian's at work, darling, I've told you.'

'But who's Brian working *for*?' said George, taking off his glasses again and squeezing the bridge of his nose.

'Abbey National, I've told you!' said Fiona. 'Ooh, I love that thing you do with your nose.'

'Mmm ... I think Brian may have been turned,' said George grimly. 'Bradford's been on to him. So's Bingley.'

'Darling,' said Fiona. 'Get under the blankets. Do that thing where you pretend to be a mole.'

George took off his glasses – yet again – and did as he was told, without committing himself.

'That's heaven,' called out Fiona. 'And how is it for you, George?'

'I really couldn't say,' said Smiley, getting up and putting on his hat. 'I have to go now. My wife telephoned. We're taking the children to the Circus.'

D. H. LAWRENCE

submits a treatment for a Carry On *film*

————————◄○►————————

The proposed *Carry On Mining* is a story for the cinemato-graph in which the principal characters feel their souls ground down in the industrial valleys of the Midlands. Sir Rodney Longpiece (to be played by Mr Sidney James) is a man whose spirit is coarsened by the fear of Bolshevism and by the carnal demands of Lady Jane, played by Miss Harriet Jacques. An itinerant Polish worker called Bustier Brazoff (to be played by Miss Katie Price) arrives in Cokeby seeking work in the mines. The foreman is a degenerate type of the mincing kind of man, played by Mr Kenneth Williams; he asks Miss Brazoff to work his most dangerous shaft. A young miner called John Thomas, to be played by Mr James Dale, takes Miss Brazoff for a country walk, where she catches her first glimpse of Aaron's rod. Afterwards they spend the night in a hayrick by an old farm. But John Thomas is appalled by the experience, the paucity of so functional an act, the miserable drip of the life force, and feels himself a soul wretched almost to hopeless-ness. His loins and nerves are tied up in shame and his bowels are moved with pity.

Angered by this response, Bustier Brazoff walks into a snowdrift to die, not knowing that she is with child by John Thomas. He next day applies to Sir Rodney Longpiece, the mine owner, for a job above ground among the hyacinths and the bluebells in the first tight buds of spring in his longing to find the soul of the old England through the queer thwarted clumsiness of his spiritual relations. Alas, Sir Sidney is away on business, but John Thomas is welcomed by the enthusiastic Lady Jane round the Tradesmen's Entrance, where she happily instructs him in his new duties.

BEDTIME STORIES

ALLEN GINSBERG
writes a Bedtime Collage, for children

I have seen Humpty Dumpty in Bellevue Hospital where
      doctors
        In white masks with electroshock try to put him
        together again

I have seen Miss Muffet ride a boxcar out of Denver past
      empty lots
        And diner backyards while the ghosts of Whitman
        and Pound
        Smoke marijuana from the ashcans and sit beside her
        tuffet

I have seen Jack Horner strung out on Benzedrine in a
      coldwater flat
        Beneath the El, begging nickels from the Buddha

I have seen Danton and Baudelaire crawling on the stoops of
      Bowery
        Fire-escapes to read the I-Ching in Fugazzi's to an
        Audience of three blind mice

I have sung all night in Luna Park where Bo Peep naked
with a baseball mitt
Dove from a pea-green rowboat with a cat who
thought he was an owl

I've been wasted all night in the Village Vanguard where
Little Boy Blue
Came blow up his horn with Coltrane and Lester Young

I have seen Old King Cole pursued by fiddlers three in
straitjackets hymning
Cuban revolution to the tune of Nature Boy – or maybe
it was *Nat* King Cole

In Atlantic City I have met a man who wasn't there. We
hitchhiked ten days
Through Nevada, living on Wild Turkey bourbon
and grits. He wasn't
There again today when we made love by the light of
the Nickelodeon in Reno.
America, America, one day you'll put a cow over the
fucking moon.
America, America, one day you'll put a cow over the
moon.

WILLIAM SHAKESPEARE

writes a speech for Basil Fawlty

—◄◦►—

Good morrow, Major, what news of battles past,
Reunions, oft-told tales and regimental ties?
(*aside*) The man's a fool and deaf as Lethe's soundless
Waters sunk in sempiternal tacitude.
Ah, Ladies, must you be gone so soon upon
Your trysts and messages? Haply the charabanc
Awaits without. Sirrah, good morrow, the room
Is not to taste? The prospect circumscrib'd,
The lodging cabin'd, cribb'd, confin'd? Pray tell
Me, sir, exactly what your fancy had envisag'd.
A wood near Athens, the bright Illyrian shore,
Or Arden's forest dense, pack'd e'en unto
Its utmost bound with prancing unicorns?
Manuel, philosopher and sage of the Iberian
Coast, pray take in charge our noble friend,
Explain – as best thy tongue may serve –
The virtues of our hostelry, its charms—
But hark! What ghastly shrieking rends the morning
Air? 'Basil! Basil!' My poisoned posset, verucca
Of my heart, she-witch of wither'd dugs and venom
For her mother's milk. I come, I come, my bride!
May Aphrodite's chariot speed me to thy side.

HANS CHRISTIAN ANDERSEN

tells a modern fairy tale

A little boy called Hans lived in a tiny crooked house in a crowded city. The landlord was the King's cruel nephew. Hans worked as a cobbler making shoes for all the rich people. One day an old witch came in and said, 'Would you like to *own* your tiny crooked house and not pay horrid rent to the King's cruel nephew?' Little Hans was thrilled. He clapped his hands and danced. The Old Witch lent him sixty crowns to buy his house and he promised to repay two crowns each year and signed his name on a piece of paper.

And that piece of paper was stolen by a Jackdaw, who gathered lots of other paper promises and made them all into a nest in the hawthorn. Then the Eagle came and said, 'I will buy your paper promises and sell them sight unseen to a Goose who cannot read.'

And the Eagle told the Goose, 'There is no risk because the Wise Owl says so. Look, he's rated them A*.'

'Thank you,' said the Goose and sold the promises to birds all over the world. And some birds wrote insurances that the promises would not fail and sold the insurance policies as well.

Meanwhile, back in the crowded city, the Old Witch rapped on Hans's door one morning. 'From now on,' she said, 'you must pay back not two crowns a year but *ten* crowns.'

And little Hans worked night and day but couldn't make enough shoes. He went blind and his hands fell off and the Old Witch said he must leave his house at once. And Hans became a beggar and wandered the world for a year in rags.

And when one day he came back to his crowded city he saw that everyone was out of work and no one had a house or a job.

Except the Old Witch and the Jackdaw and the Eagle and the Goose and the Wise Owl, who now owned the whole street, tax free.

STEPHENIE MEYER

has a Twilight *rethink and sets her school in England*

———————◄○►———————

When my mom left my dad in Phoenix, Arizona, he couldn't manage so he sent me to this school in Europe which is in England someplace. It's called Greyfriars and at the end of class none of the kids go home but they stay in a like, dorm. I'm not allowed to keep my Chevy here; can you believe the kids don't have cars? We don't do Math or Trig or Government class, we do Latin which is like what people spoke a zillion years ago in Greece or somewhere. The teacher, Mr Quelch, he's always on about some poet guy called Horace, I don't know if that's his first name or what.

There's a group of kids here who keep themselves apart, they're kind of creepy. There's Bob Cherry, who has like the biggest feet in class. There's Huree Jamset Ram Singh who's like this ethnic guy who speaks weird, I think it may be Latin, though not as weird as this kid out of Chinatown called Wun Lung.

But the one who really freaks me out is this guy called Bunter. I am like so totally in awe of him. He can like do voices, ventriloquism, shit like that. He has these thick glasses and his eyes change colour behind them. I think he reads my mind.

I think maybe he's a little shy around women, but he told me last night he loves the . . . smell of me. He said I smell of like . . . shepherd's pie and jam roly poly.

About three things I am like totally positive. First, Billy Bunter will eat anything. Second, I am unconditionally and totally in love with him. Thirdly, there's a part of him – and I don't yet know how potent it is – that wants to put me in his tuck box for what he calls a 'midnight feast'.

Sylvia Plath

tells the story of Goldilocks

I am the doctor who takes
The temperature of each bowl.

Daddy Bear, your gruel,
Grey as the Feldgrau,
Pungent as a jackboot,
Rises under an ailing moon.
I have been sleeping
In your bed, Daddy.

Mother's oats are blebbed
With ruby stains of fruit preserve
Beside the glass fire
Of her blood-orange juice.

The baby's porridge bubbles
With a foetus eye.
I swallow the sins it is not
His to shrive. I devour
The cancerous pallor
With spoons of handled bone.

I plough the winding-sheets
Of each bear bed with my
Surgical breathing, as I die and rise
Three times before dawn.

My golden hair is electric
With the light of
Borrowed stars, spread out
On my pillow of skulls.

PHILIP ROTH

turns his hand to a children's story

---◄○►---

Molestein spent the morning spring cleaning his burrow in the old Jewish district of Woodland, New Jersey. Afterwards, he had lunch with his friend Whiskers Wasserat, who lived on the waterfront at Hoboken. He and Molestein had been at college after the War on the GI Bill. They ate at Salmon's Deli. These days it was Salmon's son who cooked, but he still made mushrooms with the red sauce like his father. Molestein himself knew how to make a proper burrow, like his great grandfather who had burrowed all the way from Lithuania.

Molestein had an imaginary friend called Rutterman who was having an affair with Wasserat's 21-year-old daughter, Miriam, a dental hygienist in Newark with a fancy tail on her. Her white tunic and tan pantyhose gave Rutterman a fantasy life so rich he'd had an octuple heart bypass the previous fall.

That afternoon at Bellevue Hospital, Molestein went for a prostate exam. The geriatrician, a pop-eyed *goy* called Jimmy Toad, slipped on his rubber glove and probed the colo-rectal opening. Molestein could see the nurse, a little *shikse* ferret in a gingham pinafore, holding his discarded pants at arm's length. Dr Toad at last withdrew his probing flipper.

'Keep the news simple,' said Molestein. 'No fancy words for me or Rutterman, just the vernacular: its special force.'

'You have three months to live,' said Dr Toad, chucking his soiled glove in the trash.

Molestein went out blind onto Second Avenue. He felt the fury of his ebbing life. He thought of his elder brother, Isaac, killed while flying short-sighted night missions in Korea. Then Molestein pictured the graves of his forefathers, forgotten molehills in the forests of the remote Carpathian *shtetl*. He swore he could put Rutterman through one last trial of strength and lust for life before they shut his burrow to the light.

Awkward with his new cellphone, Molestein stopped on the corner of 58th and called Wasserat's daughter, Miriam, at the dental surgery. His voice cracked with rage and fear.

'Can you see me one more time?' said Molestein. 'It's not for me, it's for my friend Rutterman.'

'Sure, honey,' said Miriam. Her voice reminded him of gravy trickling over *kishkes*. 'There's nothing half so much fun as messing about with old goats.'

J. K. ROWLING

tries a sequel with Harry Potter now grown up

At the age of forty, Harry Potter's divorce came through. After ten years his wife Ginny was revealed to be not Ron Weasley's sister but the reincarnation of Princess Tangerina, high priestess of the Evil Mingers. Naturally, in the settlement Ginny got the kids and the house and Harry had no place to live so passed his day in the local café trying to write his memoirs till the owner kicked him out.

Eventually, desperate for a bed, he went to the local estate agent, Malvolius Slime, who sounded like a good chap, he thought, oddly.

'There's no mortgages available,' explained Malvolius, 'and with your equity, you're looking at a broom cupboard, tops. Actually this one's just come in at Number 4 Privet Drive.'

'Gazumper and gazunder!' exclaimed Harry. 'Quis circumambit circumvenit. What goes around comes—'

'I know what it means,' broke in Malvolius. 'In fact, I know all about your true history, Harry. I look like an estate agent but actually I'm one seventh of Albus Dumbledore's ghost.'

'Really?' said Harry.

'Now for the truth,' said Malvolius, promisingly. 'Hermione Grainger's pussy cat, Tarantella, is your godmother. Your parents are—'

'I know who my parents are,' replied Harry. 'And I'm an only child.'

'No,' contradicted Malvolius, testily, 'you are one of three brothers. The first is called Ant, the second is called Dec.'

'Really? Which is older?' said Harry, quizzically.

'No one knows,' said the old estate agent. 'Not even Dec. Your father – your *real* father, I should say, was Saddam Hussein. And your mother—'

'Who?' asked Harry, interrogatively. 'Who was she?'

'Your mother,' disclosed Malvolius confidentially, 'was Diana, Princess of Wales.'

'Blimey!' swore Harry, blasphemously. 'That's straining credulity a bit, isn't it? You mean my parents were . . . were Muggles?' he asked, incredulously.

'It's a long story,' said Malvolius, at length.

'How long?' said Harry, curiously.

'About seven volumes,' said Malvolius Slime, 'each one seemingly a little longer than the one before.'

* Martin McGuinness was indeed appointed minister for education in Northern Ireland.